the STORY of ChooChoo ZIMBATTÉ King of the Squishy Ishy's

M.J. LOCKWOOD

ILLUSTRATED BY DIERDRE "MS DEE" DASSEN

The Story of Choo Choo Zimbatte King of Squishy Ishy's

Copyright © 2021 by M.J. Lockwood

First Edition

Hardcover ISBN: 978-1-63837-385-8
Paperback ISBN: 978-1-63837-386-5
eBook ISBN: 978-1-68515-415-8

Each morning day, as the dew wets the plains, King Choo Choo arises, whether it Suns or it rains.

King Choo Choo is loved, more than water loves fishy's. He reigns as King, over the noble Squishy Ishy's.

The Ishy's Praise Choo Choo loudly, "we give you a cheer", because the King has provided year after year.

CHOO CHOO ZIMBATE GAVE EACH SQUISHY A LATTE, HE READ ALL THEM BOOKS AND TAUGHT THEM KARATE.

NOT ONLY DID CHOO CHOO GIVE ALL THE ISHY'S HUGS, HE BOUGHT THEM ALL CURTAINS AND FANCY NEW RUGS!

HE GAVE THEM MASSAGES, ON BACKS AND ON FEET, HE COOKED THEM CHOICE DINNER, WHITE FISH AND RED MEAT.

King Choo Choo was tired from spreading his wealth, thought he might take a few dollars, and spend on himself.

Zimbate the King, went shopping a bunch, he bought t-shirts and shoes and then went to lunch.

HE BOUGHT DIAMONDS AND SWEATPANTS,
AND A BRAND NEW JET PACK, THE SPENDING
WAS CRAZY, THIS IS A TRUE FACT.

IT DIDN'T STOP THERE, OH NO YOU SEE
WHY? KING CHOO CHOO COULDN'T STOP,
HE JUST NEEDED TO FLY.

King Choo Choo Zimbate, bought an airplane and boat, not to mention the new castle, complete with a moat.

King Choo Choo laid happy on his new golden floor, until he was bothered by a knock on the door.

It was one of the Ishy's, come to visit the King, with not so good news, not one good thing.

The Ishy explained how things had got rough, from cold dinners, no lattes, and all kinds of bad stuff.

THE ISHY STOOD FIRMLY, IN FRONT OF ZIMBATE , CLUTCHING HIS CURTAINS AND AN EMPTY FOAM LATTE.

"I KNOW YOU'RE THE BOSS AND RUN THIS WHOLE SHOW, BUT I MUST BE HONEST KING CHOO CHOO YOU ARE NOT IN THE KNOW.

OUR RUGS ARE NOT PRETTY AND THE CURTAINS ARE OLD, THE KARATE IS OUTDATED AND THE BOOKS HAVE NEW MOLD.

IF YOU DON'T WANT TO SHARE AND TAKE CARE OF YOUR PEOPLE, GIVE US RESPECT AND TREAT US AS EQUAL.

WE WILL LEAVE THIS GREAT LAND AND FIND A NEW LEADER, ONE WHO KNOWS KUNG-FU AND IS A GOOD READER".

KING CHOO CHOO SAT BACK, COULDN'T
BELIEVE HIS OWN EARS, HOW BAD THAT
HE'S BEEN, SHEDDING MULTIPLE TEARS.

"ONE MORE THING" SAID THE ISHY, GETTING READY TO LEAVE, PACKING HIS BAGS AND ROLLING HIS SLEEVE.

HE CHOKED ON HIS WORDS AND HELD BACK A CRY, "HAPPINESS IS FREE, IT'S NOT SOMETHING YOU BUY".

"HAPPINESS DOESN'T FLY FIRST CLASS
AND DOESN'T DRIVE 10-SPEED, IT JUST
NEEDS KIND HEARTS AND A GOOD BOOK
TO READ."

King Choo Choo looked round at all his possessions, took a deep breath and prepared for confessions.

"I've lost my good people, the noblest Ishy's, may I have a last request, one last ishy wishy."

The Ishy did nod and granted the plea, "I'll listen to you and I'll charge you no fee."

King Choo Choo spoke quick, "Take all that you need, for I realize now, in spite of my greed, that the Squishy's are my people, and therefore take heed, I will prove a good leader, a leader to lead."

The King did as he said and the Ishy's stood round, deciding to leave Choo Choo or stay in the town.

KING CHOO CHOO AROSE,
ON TOP OF A HILL, HOLDING
THOUSANDS OF LATTES, A
MAN OF STRONG WILL.

DROVE DOWN OFF THE HILL TOP, WITH
MORE THAN JUST COFFEE, HE BROUGHT
LEATHER BOOKS THAT SMELLED OF
SWEET TOFFEE.

BAGS AND BOXES OF GENEROUS GIFTS,
MEANT FOR THE GOOD PEOPLE, THE
SQUISHY'S OF ISH.

The Ishy's all gathered and saw all the presents, these are simple people, with the needs of small peasants.

Ignored all the trappings and lattes that came, got close to King Choo Choo and chanted his name.

THE ISHY'S ACCEPTED KING CHOO CHOO, BACK TO THEIR HOME, AND KING CHOO CHOO WAS HAPPY, BECAUSE HE WASN'T ALONE.

KING CHOO CHOO ZIMBATE LEARNED A FEW GOOD LESSONS, ASIDE FROM ALL HIS MONEY AND ALL HIS POSSESSIONS.

HE LOVED THE ISHY'S, WITH ALL OF HIS HEART, COULDN'T BEAR SEEING THEM HURT AND BEING APART. MADE RIGHT ON HIS MISTAKE, AND STILL TO THIS DAY, RULES OVER THE ISHY'S, THE FAIR AND JUST WAY.

The end.